A Note fron

The South Africa I grew up in was a warped society. The white government passed laws which separated people according to the colour of their skin. Whites were the most privileged. Indians and people of mixed race were less well off. Black people were the poorest and had the fewest rights.

When I finished school, I was called up to do army service. But I managed to avoid that by leaving the country and coming to live in England. Years later, I began to write stories about the people I had known who had been affected by the unjust laws.

South Africa now is a very different place, with equal rights and opportunities for all. But racism has a nasty way of creeping into any country, and into anyone's mind. It is a great challenge to find a way of living which is free of prejudice against other people.

Contents

Mr Naidoo's Hundredth

Birthday

Chapter 1

The Handyman

In my last year at school I had a Saturday morning job at Valhalla Furniture Store. I worked mainly in the lighting department, demonstrating various lamps and light fittings for customers.

My head was so filled with details of watts and volts, I'm sure it would have shone in the dark like strobe lights.

Naturally, I didn't do this job out of choice – I had better things to do on a Saturday morning than bringing light into other people's lives. But my dad insisted I worked in the store. And it was because of him that I got paid almost nothing. But what could I do about it? He owned Valhalla Furniture.

Working in the store I got to know old Boola, the handyman, quite well. I think you have to put yourself in someone else's skin before you can understand them properly, don't you think? All the more so if their skin is a different colour to yours.

At any rate, that's what my ma always says about the disabled people she works with at the Woltemade Centre.

Old Boola had been a handyman at Valhalla Furniture for years – he was quite good with a hammer and nails and a saw. All the furniture assembly and that sort of thing was left to Boola. But he also fancied himself as a smooth-talking salesman, and was always trying to get a piece of the sales action.

I think he reckoned he could talk a man with no wife into buying a double bed, but as far as I know, the closest he ever came to that was talking some old sailor into buying a rocking chair to remind him of the ocean waves.

My ma always took time to talk to Boola, on her brief visits to Valhalla Furniture. "How's Meena doing?" she would ask every time she came into the store.

I suppose my ma was interested in Boola's daughter Meena because of her work with disabled people.

From what I could gather, Meena was a bit slow.

"She's OK, Missus, but she struggles coping with the children, you know."

"Is it four children?"

"It's five now, Missus."

"That's a shame," my ma would say. "What about a husband for her?"

"No, Missus, the men just take advantage of her. They don't want to marry someone like her, even though she's got a heart of gold, I tell you."

"Can't you arrange a marriage for her?" my ma asked.

"I've tried, Missus, but the only man I could get had a messed-up face."

"What do you mean?" Ma persisted.

"He was in a car accident and his face was very bad. No woman would look at him."

"Did Meena meet him?"

"Yes, Missus. She said he was a nice man, very kind, and she would marry him. But after he spoke to her, he said to me he didn't want to marry a halfwit person."

"What a shame," my ma said.

Boola struggled hard to support Meena and her five children. He lived with them in a little house in the back of the Retreat District.

I suppose that's why he tried hard to get in on the sales action to earn a bit of extra money.

Chapter 2

Bankrupt

It became harder and harder to sell anything at Valhalla Furniture. Even the real salesmen were having trouble.

It was all the fault of the Discount Centre opposite. The trouble started up when the huge Newgate shopping precinct got built across the road from Valhalla Furniture. For three years my dad had to watch those guys build up their business, while the same guys watched him going down the drain.

But the Discount Centre was ruthless. They took back your furniture if you didn't pay your instalments on the dot. You could see their heavies going out in their brand new vans and returning to the Centre with the almost-new furniture.

My dad did his debt-collecting mostly on his own. One Saturday morning he took me with him.

I sat in our trusty, old van as he knocked on the front door of a tin-roofed house. A huge man with a red face came to the door and I heard my dad explaining the situation to him. But he couldn't have explained it very well, because the red-faced chap started waving his enormous hands about.

"A man's got to eat!" he yelled.

I thought what a pity my dad had disturbed him during his meal.

"You think all I've got to do is pay you for that crap table you sold us? Come in and see it, man, it's falling to bits."

I wasn't surprised. If he thrashed about with his hands like that at mealtimes the table wouldn't have stood a chance. Neither would my dad's face, if he argued much longer.

"I didn't want that table in the first place. It's your salesman who told me I needed to eat on a dining table. There was nothing wrong with my old kitchen table. If you can't wait another month for your money, you can take back your crap dining table and I'll tell you where you can shove it."

Well, of course, in the end my dad was persuaded by these powerful words and all that hand-waving. He took pity on the man and left him to finish his dinner. I don't know if he ever got paid for that table.

Meanwhile, the owners of the Discount Centre opposite got richer and richer.

Even our regular customers started buying their furniture from them. My dad would surely have developed stomach ulcers if he'd gone on watching such ruthless men make a fortune while his own business went to the dogs.

But he soon went bankrupt. It all happened very quickly and was over and done with in a jiffy. Soon after, my dad got a job at the Plaza cinema, and he's never looked back. He's always loved films and knows who acts in every one and who wrote the music and who directed it and so on.

At the time Valhalla Furniture was getting into trouble, Boola was very anxious about losing his job. "Who will look after my daughter and my grandchildren, Boss?" he asked my dad.

My dad had no answer. Who's going to employ a shabbily dressed, 63-year-old Indian whose smooth-talking mouth dribbles saliva every now and again?

The last straw at Valhalla was the burglary. There had been a whole lot of shop burglaries in the area and my dad was seriously worried, because he knew Valhalla didn't have modern security alarms.

In fact, it didn't have any security alarms at all. My dad had just stretched some wires across the shop windows himself, to look like a proper burglar alarm system. But the wires all went to this fake red box that he found somewhere, and that wasn't plugged into anything! He had even got hold of a metal sign to hang outside the store. It read THIS PROPERTY IS PROTECTED BY TRIDENT SECURITY SYSTEMS.

This trick had obviously worked for the seven years my dad owned Valhalla Furniture, because it had never been burgled. He also had a lot of faith in the fact that the police station was just down the road.

But *these* burglars must have had no respect for the police being so close. And they weren't fooled by the fake sign either. They stole thousands of rands' worth of goods, mostly small furniture items, light fittings and rugs – it must have been well-planned. They even stole the metal Trident Security Systems sign.

My dad lost a lot of money, because the insurance company wouldn't pay up once they discovered my dad's so-called security system was fake. It was an awful morning, standing there in a half-empty shop, realising that the end had come. And it was even more awful knowing the people from the Discount Centre across the road were watching and gloating at our misfortune.

But Boola wasn't working there any more when the end came.

Chapter 3

Boola's Life Story

It's funny, now I look back on all the time Boola worked for my dad, I would never have guessed that he was the sort of person to do what he did. Even though once or twice I spoke to him about his life.

I remember once old Boola asked me about the Woltemade Centre where my ma worked.

I think maybe he secretly wanted to know if they could help his daughter, Meena, in any way.

I told him that the Centre was named after a bloke called Wolraad Woltemade. A long time ago he rode out into the raging waves to save the lives of some sailors who were shipwrecked in Table Bay. Time after time he rode out into the sea, returning with desperate sailors clinging to his horse. Until his horse grew tired and both man and beast sank beneath the waves.

"That's a smart story, Master Basil," Boola said. "You will be a good journalist. Then you must tell a smart story about me, hey?"

"What must I tell?"

"You can tell that Boola got through two years at High School. Then he worked for 25 years for Mr Swersky selling bicycles and 18 years for Mr Leopold making picture frames.

Then he worked for another seven years for your dad in the furniture trade."

"That's not enough for a story," I said.

"Man," said Boola. "It was enough for a life. Why not for a story?"

"Didn't anything interesting ever happen to you?"

"Of course, what do you think I am? Now let me remember."

But old Boola's memory wasn't that good, I reckon, because the best he could come up with was something about marrying some no-good girl who ran off with a black man, leaving him with a simple-minded daughter.

"And I've got good Indian and Malay blood in me," he told me angrily. "Not like that piece of rubbish she ran off with!"

But on that occasion, I never guessed what Boola had done. Nor did I guess another time long ago, when I must have been about 12 or so, and Boola helped me with my woodwork project for school.

I had decided to make a wooden jigsaw puzzle with this great picture I had – well, really it was a poster – of surfers. I stuck it onto some plywood with glue, then drew the outlines of all the pieces of the jigsaw on the back. But my attempts at using the fret saw were hopeless.

"You can't use such a blunt blade!" Boola told me, when I showed him my efforts. "This blade is as smooth as a baby's bum."

It looked sharp enough to me, but he ran his leathery, old thumb over the blade to prove the point.

So I went to the hardware shop and bought a new pack of blades.

"This is how you use a fret saw," Boola said. "You keep the blade moving steady like this, see, and you keep the blade nice and upright."

I tried, but still my jigsaw pieces chipped as I turned the corners.

In the end, Boola did half of the sawing and I did the other half. "Hey, that's great handiwork, hey!" he grinned.

The jigsaw was fantastic. There were 200 pieces of complicated puzzle, which would give anybody a hard time.

My teacher liked my work and gave me a good mark. Much better than the mark I got for making my Perspex matchbox holder the year before.

Yes, looking back, it was easy to see that, even while Boola was helping me with that jigsaw, I really didn't know anything about the man who was sitting there.

Chapter 4
A Birthday Visit

I only found out what sort of person Boola really was when two men turned up one day at the lighting department at Valhalla Furniture.

"We're from the City of Cape Town," one man said. He was dressed in a smart, grey business suit. "We're looking for someone called Mr Gopal Naidoo."

"No-one called Mr Gopal Naidoo works here," I said. "I've never heard of him."

"Are you sure?" the other man asked. His suit was dark blue, and he was carrying a box wrapped in shiny, gold paper. "Where's the manager of this place?"

"My dad's the manager," I said. "Come with me."

As they walked behind me, Mr Grey was whispering to Mr Blue. "You see, I told you he couldn't be at this place. He's too old to be working anywhere. That woman we spoke to was half-witted. She didn't even know her own name."

When we reached my dad's office, he told them that there was no Mr Gopal Naidoo working in the store. Only a Mr Boola Naidoo.

Mr Blue raised his eyebrows. "Did Mr Naidoo work in the Parks Department?" he asked.

"I doubt it," my dad said. "He's been a handyman for years. I don't think he knows the first thing about gardening."

"The Mr Gopal Naidoo that we're looking for didn't work as a gardener," Mr Blue explained. "He worked as a cleaner."

"We'd better have a word with this Mr Boola Naidoo!" Mr Grey said.

Boola came into the office, smiling and showing his brown teeth.

"Are you Mr Boola Naidoo?" Mr Grey asked him.

"That's me," Boola answered.

"Do you know a Mr Gopal Naidoo?" Mr Blue asked.

"Yes, sir, that's my father."

"Excellent," Mr Blue said. "We have been trying to find him. We've got an address in Retreat for him, but when we got there, this woman we spoke to told us he wasn't there, and we should try Valhalla Furniture. Do you know where we can find him?"

"Why do you want to see him?" Boola asked.

"We understand the old boy is 100 years old today," Mr Grey explained, "so we have come to give him this gift and a certificate signed by the Mayor of Cape Town himself."

"Thank you," Boola said. "I will give it to him."

"That's good of you, but we need to have a photograph of your father receiving the award."

"My father is not well," Boola said. "He's very ill. He cannot have his photograph taken at the moment."

"I'm sorry he's not well," Mr Grey said. "But where is he?"

Boola looked as if he was trying to sell a double bed to a man with no wife. "He's ... he's ... he's at my brother's house in Port Elizabeth," he told them.

"So when he claims his pension every month," Mr Grey said, "why does he give the address in Retreat?"

"Because ... because ..." Boola wasn't having any luck selling his double bed. "Because he always lives in Retreat except now when he is so ill. I send the money on to him in Port Elizabeth."

Mr Grey turned again to Mr Blue. "There's some funny business going on here, don't you think?"

"Yes, I smell a rat," Mr Blue answered.

"Look here, Mr Naidoo, the City of Cape Town has been paying out a pension to Mr Gopal Naidoo for 35 years. For 35 years he has put his thumbprint on our claim forms.

"According to our records, he is 100 years old today. So we've come to pay him the respects of the City of Cape Town and to give him this nice box of gifts and a certificate. But if he's in Port Elizabeth, then can you tell me how he's been filling in his claim form?"

Poor old Boola didn't know what to say.

"It's a serious offence to forge a pension claim," Mr Blue said.

"But what about the thumbprint?" my father said. "You can't forge a thumbprint."

"I think we'll take another ride to that house in Retreat," Mr Grey said, "and this time you can come with us, Mr Naidoo."

Old Boola bowed his head pathetically and went off with the two men.

"I can't leave the store," my dad said to me. "But let's see if we can get hold of your ma."

He made a quick phone call. Within ten minutes my ma had collected me and we were off to Retreat to see if Boola needed help.

Once we found the street, it was easy to see which was Boola's house. It was the one with the shiny, black Ford parked outside. It had the City of Cape Town crest painted on its door.

We knocked on the door. It was opened by a short, plump woman in a shabby, worn-out, pink dress. "Yes Boola is here," she said, in a sweet child's voice. "But he is talking to two men."

"We want to talk to him too, Meena," my ma said, taking her confidently by the arm and leading her indoors.

Chapter 5
The Jar

Boola's house was very small, just a front room and two back rooms and a kitchen. Two barefoot children were sitting on the floor of the front room, their noses runny and their clothes ragged.

On the wall behind the couch was a faded picture of the Hindu elephant god with his many arms. The couch itself was covered with a large, shabby cloth, that might once have been an old curtain. Boola was sitting on it. He was so upset he could hardly greet my ma.

I could hear the voices of Mr Grey and Mr Blue coming from one of the back rooms.

Meena sat down next to Boola. My ma and me kept standing.

"Why are those men looking in the back room, Boola?" Meena asked him.

"They're just looking for papers," Boola said.

Suddenly, the two men emerged. Mr Grey was triumphantly holding up a jar in his hands, well away from his nose, which appeared to be suffering from the effects of some foul smell.

If they were surprised to see my ma and me in the house, they didn't show it. Mr Grey just held up the jar and I could see it contained liquid.

"I'd like you to meet what is left of the 100-year-old Mr Gopal Naidoo!" Mr Grey said, giving us a closer look at the jar.

I couldn't believe it.

There, swimming in the liquid, was an ancient, old thumb.

The thumb of Mr Gopal Naidoo, Boola's father, who had died 20-something years ago.

My ma remained silent.

Boola held his head down. He knew he was in big trouble.

"This is a serious offence, Mr Naidoo," Mr Blue said. "You will be hearing from us and the police in due course."

Mr Grey and Mr Blue strutted off, pleased with their day's work.

"What was in the bottle, Boola?" Meena asked.

"It was our life's savings," Boola answered gently, putting his arm around her.

DOUBLE VISION

Chapter 1
Going Mad

When did I first start going mad? I don't know.

The idea came to me slowly at first, but then gathered speed as I got to my final year at school and the day of being called up to do army service got nearer.

I used to practise going mad quite a lot. "One of my eyes sees one thing, and the other eye sees something quite different," I used to say.

"What are you talking about, Basil, for God's sake?" my ma would say.

"One eye sees people, even women and children, with their skulls crushed," I explained. "And the other eye sees people having a picnic on the beach with cold chicken sandwiches."

I got the idea of going mad from chameleons. I used to find them on the branches of bushes and take them home in a bottle.

When I was younger and belonged to the school nature club, I used to be keen on wildlife. Hyenas, cheetahs, rhinos, warthogs – you name it, I used to know all about them.

Not that I ever saw these creatures live, of course, except in the zoo. I probably would have run a mile if a hyena or a warthog came prowling anywhere near me. But I had lots of postcards of these animals.

The only real wildlife I ever came across was ladybugs, lizards, spiders, scorpions and chameleons. Chameleons were my favourite, because you could let them walk up your arms and feed them flies.

A chameleon's tongue is as long as its head and body put together – not counting its tail – and this tongue is sticky. It was good fun to put a fly quite far from the chameleon's mouth and watch that tongue shoot out and scoop up its prey.

Another thing you could do with a chameleon was to put it on different coloured objects and see it change colour. A chameleon can change from its usual green to a dark reddish-grey or to a lighter sort of creamy green – it's something to do with its eyes being sensitive to differences in colour – but I think it changes most when it's afraid.

The weirdest thing of all, though, is the way a chameleon's eyes work. Each moves independently of the other, so that one eye can be fixed on one thing way over on the left and the other eye is rolling around looking for something else. It's mad.

"One eye sees people in uniforms beating up and killing other people, the other sees people playing cricket or rugby together at Newlands."

"You're a bit crazy, you know that, Basil?" my ma would say, putting her palm flat on my forehead to see if I had a high temperature.

Of course, that one trick wasn't going to be enough to persuade anyone but my ma that I was going crazy.

So I checked through our Family Health book and came up with this mental illness called schizophrenia, which can sometimes affect teenagers. They start to live in their own fantasy world.

"I keep hearing this voice, Ma."

"Basil, what are you talking about, for God's sake?"

"This man keeps telling me things."

"What things?"

"He tells me that prison is not the best place to spend the next six years."

"Who tells you this?"

"I don't know who he is. I think he's old, maybe a godfather or something."

"You haven't got a godfather, Basil."

"Well, he sounds like a godfather. At least he's interested in my life."

I soon ran out of details from the Family Health book and went to the library to search through other books on schizophrenia. What a pity I had burnt the book on the human body which my parents had given me in the hope I would become a doctor. It had a good chapter on mental illness.

"This man talks to me day and night, Ma. I don't know any more if I'm dreaming or if I'm awake. He keeps telling me how horrible prison is."

"Why does he talk about prison? You're not going to prison," Ma said.

"He says I mustn't go into the army either. And it's six years in prison for not going."

"Who's been putting these ideas into your head, Basil? Is it your friend Jonathan Levy down the road? I always thought he was too political."

"No, Ma. Jonathan hardly ever talks to me. It's my godfather."

"But why doesn't he want you to go into the army, for goodness sake?" Ma demanded to know.

"Because he doesn't want me to, that's why. He doesn't want me mutilating people's bodies or killing them. He wants me to become a priest."

"What kind of priest?"

"A Christian priest. He says I would make a good priest or a monk."

My ma wasn't pleased with this as we were supposed to be a Jewish family. "Are you making this up, Basil?"

"No, Ma, I'm not. I wish you could listen in through my one ear, then you'd hear him talking. He's got a loud voice. Do you want to try?"

I don't know what got into me saying something as stupid as that. I remember when I was eight or nine and my friend Dewie had pins and needles, I told him it was catching.

"You can't catch pins and needles!" our teacher told me.

"Yes, you can," I said, and I put my knee against Dewie's knee for a few seconds.

"There! I've caught them!" I said. "My knee's got pins and needles now too."

Our teacher shook her head – as if I was crazy.

That was ten years ago.

My ma has a history of depression and she spent a month in a clinic after my granny's leg had to be amputated. But she wasn't so crazy now that she'd try to listen to the voice inside my head.

When I began to starve myself, my dad started losing patience.

"You'd better stop this nonsense, Basil. People will say I've got a mad son."

"What do people matter? None of them are equal," I said. "My godfather says I shouldn't live in this world. He says I should go to another world where everyone is equal."

Then my dad got angry. "You tell your communist godfather not to put such ridiculous ideas into your head. The only world where everyone is equal is Heaven and that exists only in the minds of madmen. This here is the *real* world, you tell your godfather, with *real* flesh and blood people. And we're all different, but we still have to share the same world somehow, even if a few people get hurt now and then."

"My godfather says that Heaven sounds like a nice place, even if only madmen live there."

"Yes, well, you tell your godfather, the way you're going, you'll soon be in a place where only madmen live."

"That's a good place for a priest," I said.

That was when my dad really laid into me. He said he would disown me if I went anywhere near the Christian religion.

Chapter 2

Convincing the Doctor

As my madness got worse, I stopped wearing my uniform to school. I wore a red tie with little, pink stars instead of the blue-and-yellow striped tie. I wore my faded, blue denim jacket instead of the navy-blue blazer, and I wore ripped jeans instead of grey trousers, and Adidas trainers instead of my black school shoes.

A few boys laughed when I arrived at school and my teacher took me straight to the Head's office.

"Where do you think you are, Basil Kushenovitz?" the Head said. "The New Year Carnival?"

"No, sir, but this man said I must dress like this today because of the rotten state of Denmark."

I got that from reading *Hamlet*. In fact the whole idea of pretending to go mad and dressing like a weirdo came from *Hamlet*. So please blame William Shakespeare for what was happening to me.

"Did you get that from one of your English lessons?" the Head asked.

"No! There's this man who keeps talking to me. My godfather. He's the one who told me to dress like this. He said you wouldn't mind. He said you'd probably write to the army yourself and tell them I'm not fit to be a soldier."

"I always thought you were strange, Kushenovitz, but I didn't know you were round the twist."

The Head phoned my ma to collect me and she took me straight off to Dr Goldberg. That's where my studies of schizophrenia really came in handy.

After checking my pulse and looking down my throat and testing my blood pressure and knocking my knees with a hammer, he started asking me questions.

"So when did you last hear this voice?"

"About 10.15 last night," I answered. "Just after I heard the machine guns firing outside in the street."

"What machine guns?" Dr Goldberg asked.

"Didn't you hear them? I thought everyone must have heard them. The tanks were very loud."

"What tanks?"

I started to shake and shiver as I remembered the war going on outside between the South African army and the coloureds and the Indians and the blacks.

"It's all right, Basil," Dr Goldberg said, trying to calm me down.

"They were killing hundreds of people right in front of my eyes. They even crushed the skull of that girl who lives across the road."

I held my hands up over my eyes to try and forget the full horror of that scene. I bit my lip until it bled and let out this awful primitive groan of agony.

"Calm down, Basil!" Dr Goldberg said, but my visions were by now too vivid for me to do as he asked.

"With my one eye, I keep seeing people being killed. Doctor, you must tell the army I don't want to do their dirty work for them, OK?"

"All right, Basil, but first let me try to understand. What did the voice actually say to you?"

"My godfather said that I was a special person, chosen by him to become a Christian priest or monk, and no way should I go into the army. In fact, he said, I should never again wear any uniform. He said uniforms are very dangerous because they stick to your skin and then become part of your skin and you can never take them off afterwards."

"How long has your godfather been speaking to you?"

"Oh, ever since the war began," I said.

"When was that?"

"You must know," I said. "A long time ago. When I was a kid. My ears got hurt in the war."

"So you were deaf for a while? But you could still hear the voice."

Dr Goldberg was writing notes like mad, and in the end he called my ma into the room. He told her I was much too tense and stressed out from studying for my final exams and that I needed a good rest.

He mentioned that my thoughts were confused. He said I was depressed about the idea of going into the army to do my military training.

"Do you think he's inherited something from me?" my ma asked.

Poor thing, she wanted to blame herself for my troubles.

"Not at all," Dr Goldberg said. "You were just depressed. We'll see if Basil gets over this little spell if he relaxes. Take him off on a short holiday. Let him sunbathe – not in the midday sun, of course – and generally take things easy. If he's no better in three weeks, bring him back for another check-up. And get him to take these tablets. They'll help his body and mind to relax."

He handed my ma the prescription. "By the way," he said to her, "did he ever have trouble with his ears when he was young?"

"Yes, he went deaf for about a month when he was two or three years old."

Chapter 3

A Desperate Case

It wasn't possible for my dad to take time off work to go on holiday just then, so my ma said she'd just take my brother and me to the beach every day instead.

Of course, the first thing I did was to swap the tablets Dr Goldberg had prescribed for aspirin. And every day, when my ma asked if I'd taken my pills, I'd answer yes quite truthfully. Once or twice I even made a show of swallowing them in front of her.

But the day of my call-up came ever nearer. I had to go for an army medical check-up and I wasn't looking forward to it at all.

Even thinking of going anywhere near the army made my head spin.

"Ma, I don't want to be a terrorist," I pleaded.

"What are you talking about?"

"The army will train me to be a terrorist, to kill and mutilate innocent people."

My father was not at all impressed by the act I was putting on. "Best thing for Basil would be to spend some time in the army. I did army service and it made a man of me. There's nothing like army discipline to knock a boy into shape."

"But you didn't have to kill black people, did you?" I screamed at him.

"Who said you'll have to?"

"In the army you have to kill black people and women and children and mutilate their bodies and ... "

"Pull yourself together, Basil!" my father ordered. "You don't have to do any of that. They'll just get you into good physical shape and train you to march and use a rifle and to survive out in the bush ..."

"And to cut off people's ears and noses!" I screamed.

After that outburst, I screamed some more, and then again, so that finally my father phoned Dr Goldberg and made another appointment for me. Ma came with me.

"Has he been taking the tablets?" Dr Goldberg asked.

"Yes, he has," my ma answered.

"And they've had no effect?" he asked.

"For the first few days he improved. But now I think he's getting much worse."

"Well, well, well," Dr Goldberg said. "I think it's time we had some specialist advice on the matter. The man to see is Dr Perlman. He will be able to recommend some sort of therapy. But it will be six or eight weeks before you can see him. He's a busy man."

"I can't wait that long!" I shouted, grabbing hold of the stethoscope that was hanging round Dr Goldberg's neck. "In six or eight weeks I could be up at the frontier, murdering people or I could be in the townships mutilating children. The uniform could stick to my skin and then how would I ever get it off?"

But Dr Perlman refused to believe that I was a desperate case, so I had to wait for seven weeks to see him.

Chapter 4

The Army Medical

Before I got to see Dr Perlman, the day of my army medical arrived. There were hundreds of other suckers just like me, but they didn't seem too bothered.

The sergeant, or whatever he was, thought he'd give us a taste of the army in advance and he shouted out his command for us all to get undressed. "Fully undressed, hey! And that means taking off your filthy underpants, understand?"

I waited in this long queue until I arrived at the desk of the army doctor.

"Basil Kushy-what? Kushy-what-the-hell? How do you say your name?"

He checked my pulse, looked down my throat, tested my blood pressure and hit my knees with a rubber hammer. Then he moved between my legs and squeezed my balls, and had a good look to check there were two of them, and not one or three, and that I hadn't borrowed anyone else's.

"Ever had polio, scarlet fever, malaria, jaundice, chickenpox, smallpox or letterbox?" he rattled. He made this stupid joke with everyone.

"No."

"Ever had heart trouble? And I don't mean trouble with girlfriends."

"No."

"So you're fit and ready to join the army?"

"Yes, perfectly," I said, "except for my schizophrenia."

"What's wrong with schizophrenia? I tell you, schizophrenics make the best lorry drivers in the army."

"That's OK, then," I said, "because a snake loses its skin when it's grown a new one."

"What's a snake got to do with it?"

"You know," I whispered, sort of leaning over towards his ear.

"What?" asked the army doctor.

"When the uniform sticks to me, my old skin will fall off, just like a snake, won't it? Doesn't it happen to you, sir?"

The army doctor screwed up his nose at me and gave me a hard look. "Are you trying to make fun of me, boy?"

"No, sir, not in the least, sir," I said. "But I'm so worried about shedding my skin."

"Shedding your skin?"

"Yes, sir, you know, when my skin falls off. You can't tell yet, though, can you?" I asked him.

"Tell what?"

"You know, how soon my skin will fall off. You know snakes even shed their eyes. I must protect my eyes," I explained to him.

The army doctor shook his head from side to side. A lopsided smile formed on his lips, as he looked through the folder with my notes in it.

"Your mother's been in a mental home?" he said.

"No."

"It says here she's been in a clinic."

"That's right," I said. "A clinic, not a mental home."

"What difference does a word make? She's been in a mental home. And you've been seeing Dr Goldberg about hearing voices. What voices?"

"Oh, just voices. It's nothing," I said. "Just my godfather telling me that I must be careful never to cut off anyone's nose or ears. He said it's very unhealthy for me to go round killing and mutilating children. And he also warned me only last night that if I'm not careful with what I wear I could become a coloured or an Indian or even an African. You see, if a chameleon is frightened it can change colour in a moment."

"Do you always talk this sort of crap, or is this something special you save for the army?"

"Oh no, sir, I always talk crap like this. You ask my father. He can't stand it any more. Nor my mother. Nor my brother. And I've got to go and see this specialist, called Dr Perlman, in a few weeks' time because he's a shrink and he loves listening to people who talk just like me."

"You're not putting this on, are you?" the army doctor said. "To get out of military service?"

"No way, sir. It's my godfather who told me that the question is to be or not to be. Because my trouble is that one eye sees one thing and the other eye sees something else."

I tried to look in two different directions with my two eyes. "It's like this, my one eye sees these mutilated bodies ..."

I started to shiver and shake as the images of mutilation and killing flashed through my mind. And this primitive groan escaped from my trembling lips.

"But my other eye ..."

"Give me a break! I don't think the army's going to want either of your eyes, Kushy-what-ever-your-name-is. Not until you've had some E.C.T. shock treatment. I think some strong electric current through your brain would help your eyes a lot. We will contact your doctor and we will write to you in due course informing you of our decision."

I tried to control my shaking. "My godfather will be very grateful to you, sir. But you

shouldn't wear that uniform, sir. It will stick
to your skin ..."

Barrington Stoke would like to thank all its readers for commenting on the manuscript before publication and in particular:

Stephanie Adams
Claudene Armitage
Eileen Armstrong
Nick Bull
Amanda Cant
Emma Chapman
Laura Coles
Sarah Cowan
Rebecca Cunningham
Fiona Dewar
Sarah Downie
Denise Hindmarsh

Michael Hulse
Nina Khawaja
Victoria Milward
Nicky Mitchell
Natalie Moore
Polly Nabarro
Jolinda Pollock
Chris Scott
Helen Wainwright
Liz Watson
Stacey Watson
Jason Wrightson

Become a Consultant!

Would you like to give us feedback on our titles before they are published? Contact us at the address below – we'd love to hear from you!

Barrington Stoke, 10 Belford Terrace, Edinburgh EH4 3DQ
Tel: 0131 315 4933 Fax: 0131 315 4934
E-mail: info@barringtonstoke.co.uk
Website: www.barringtonstoke.co.uk

More Teen Titles!

Joe's Story by Rachel Anderson 1-902260-70-8
Playing Against the Odds by Bernard Ashley 1-902260-69-4
Harpies by David Belbin 1-842990-31-4
Firebug by Eric Brown 1-842991-03-5
TWOCKING by Eric Brown 1-842990-42-X
To Be A Millionaire by Yvonne Coppard 1-902260-58-9
All We Know of Heaven by Peter Crowther 1-842990-32-2
The Ring of Truth by Alan Durant 1-842990-33-0
Falling Awake by Viv French 1-902260-54-6
The Wedding Present by Adèle Geras 1-902260-77-5
The Cold Heart of Summer by Alan Gibbons 1-842990-80-2
Shadow on the Stairs by Ann Halam 1-902260-57-0
Alien Deeps by Douglas Hill 1-902260-55-4
Partners in Crime by Nigel Hinton 1-842991-02-7
The New Girl by Mary Hooper 1-842991-01-9
Dade County's Big Summer by Lesley Howarth 1-842990-43-8
Runaway Teacher by Pete Johnson 1-902260-59-7
No Stone Unturned by Brian Keaney 1-842990-34-9
Wings by James Lovegrove 1-842990-11-X
A Kind of Magic by Catherine MacPhail 1-842990-10-1
Stalker by Anthony Masters 1-842990-81-0
Clone Zone by Jonathan Meres 1-842990-09-8
The Dogs by Mark Morris 1-902260-76-7
Turnaround by Alison Prince 1-842990-44-6
Dream On by Bali Rai 1-842990-45-4
All Change by Rosie Rushton 1-902260-75-9
Fall Out by Rosie Rushton 1-842990-74-8
The Blessed and The Damned by Sara Sheridan 1-842990 08-X